P
G
F

EXTREME ADVENTURES

BOOK 2

Bushfire Rescue

JUSTIN D'ATH

Kane Miller

A DIVISION OF EDC PUBLISHING

First American Edition 2010
Kane Miller, A Division of EDC Publishing

First published in 2005 by Penguin Group (Australia)
Text copyright © Justin D'Ath 2005

Kane Miller, A Division of EDC Publishing
P.O. Box 470663
Tulsa, OK 74147-0663
www.kanemiller.com
www.edcpub.com

Library of Congress Control Number: 2009931603

Printed and bound in the United States of America
1 2 3 4 5 6 7 8 9 10
ISBN: 978-1-935279-33-4

For Matisse

RUNAWAY

In the last ten or fifteen minutes something strange had happened. Everything had gone hazy. When I looked up through the gum trees, I couldn't see a single cloud from one towering ridgetop to the other. The sun was halfway up in the morning sky, yet somehow the day didn't seem as bright as it had when I'd set out from the homestead thirty minutes earlier. Weird.

Susie, the horse I was riding, had begun acting strangely, too – snorting and tossing her head and prancing sideways along the steep, narrow cattle trail. It was hard to stay in the saddle. When I pulled on the reins to slow her, the little palomino paid no attention. She knew I was only a novice rider and not in control.

"Hey, cut it out!" I cried, trying to sound confident.

It worked. Susie stopped acting up and settled into her normal bumpy trot.

I leaned forward to scratch her coarse white mane. "Good horse," I said, which showed how little I knew about horses. Then I glanced up at the sky again. A mistake. Because that was when Susie deliberately walked into an overhanging branch. I should have been expecting it. Nan Corcoran had warned me about the straw-colored mare when I volunteered to take Pop's lunch up to the high pasture, where he was fixing fences.

"Watch her, Sam," Nan had said, holding Susie steady while I swung shakily up into the saddle. "She likes being ridden, but she's full of tricks."

This trick backfired on Susie. Hardly thicker than my thumb, the branch she'd walked into wasn't big enough to sweep me off her back. It bent harmlessly out of the way. But something was attached to the branch, and *that* wasn't harmless.

Wasps' nest! warned a little voice in my head.

Too late. The gray saucer-shaped nest slapped

against my shoulder, and a cloud of angry insects exploded into the air around me. I'm allergic to bees and wasps. One sting can put me in the hospital. Three or four stings, my doctor says, and it would be all over, red rover. Luckily, I was wearing riding gloves and a long-sleeved shirt. The deadly swarm centered its attack on my hands and arms so I wasn't stung. Susie wasn't as lucky. At least two of the large yellow and black wasps attached themselves to her neck, their long stingers plunged savagely downwards, while a third flew into her left ear.

Trouble! Susie let out a loud whinny and leapt high into the air, tossing me out of the saddle. It took me by surprise. I was still fighting off the wasps; I had even let go of the reins. By some miracle I landed on Susie's back again, only now I was flat on my stomach with my arms around her neck. The mare bucked a few more times, flinging me around like a rag doll, then she broke into a gallop.

I had never ridden a galloping horse before. In my short career as a rider, I had only dared take Susie to a slow canter. Now she was going flat out. Trees shot past like matchsticks. It made me dizzy to look at them. "Try to match yourself to the horse's rhythm,"

Nan had told me on the first day of my vacation. Good advice, I'm sure, but impossible when you're lying prone along a horse's back. Susie felt like a jackhammer underneath me, pummeling my chest and stomach. She had saved me from the wasps, but now she was out to kill me.

"Whoa!" I cried, or tried to. It came out sounding like: "Woh-oh-oh-oh-oh-oh!"

Susie paid no attention. If anything, she went faster. I held on grimly. Nothing was going to make me let go. It was life or death. Nan had loaned me one of her old riding helmets, but that wouldn't help me if I hit the ground at this speed. A broken neck seemed the most likely outcome.

Suddenly the trees were gone. We had left the forest. Susie was galloping across open grassland. I saw a fence reeling past to my right, a blur of posts and wire. Susie swerved through a gate. Some holding yards flashed by, then I saw a dusty black truck with a ramp leading up into the back. A man holding a rope stood next to the ramp. A second man sat on a motorcycle ten or fifteen yards away. Between the two men stood a huge white bull. It had a rope tied around its neck. Kosciusko Rex!

Susie had taken a wrong turn; she'd brought me down to the bull paddock.

"He-e-e-e-l-l-p!" I yelled, as we shot past.

It was too late. Already the men, the bull and the truck were behind us. It didn't matter. Susie seemed to be slowing of her own accord. Since entering the paddock, her gait had changed from a gallop to a fast canter. I adjusted my grip around her neck and tried to work my body forward into the saddle. The reins flapped and danced in front of me. If I could grab hold of them, I might be able to ease the mare down to a walk.

What was that noise? The drumming of Susie's hooves drowned out most other sounds, but I could hear a high, wailing whine. It seemed to be growing louder. I glanced over my shoulder. The man on the motorcycle was racing across the wide brown paddock behind us.

"It's okay," I yelled at him. "I've got it under control."

I was worried that his noisy machine would scare Susie just when she was beginning to calm down. But the motorcycle rider couldn't hear me. He kept coming. He was fifteen yards behind me and catching up fast. I shook my head at him. I even risked letting go with one hand and waving him away. He didn't take the hint. He came up right alongside. Just as I'd feared, Susie broke into a gallop. She began veering away from the yammering motorcycle.

"Get away! You're scaring her!" I yelled.

The rider was wearing a helmet, but I could see his small, pink-rimmed eyes through the visor. They looked like the eyes of a pig.

"Yaah! Yaah! Yaah!" he shouted, forcing Susie into a sharp turn.

What was he doing? Was he trying to kill us?

Wham!

② THE JINDABYNE RUSTLERS

Like me, Susie's attention had been focused on the motorcycle. She saw the fence at the last moment. It was too late to swerve, and the fence was too high to jump. With a terrified whinny, the little mare planted all four hooves in the dusty pasture and slid straight into it. The wires absorbed the impact, and Susie bounced back like a ball off of a tennis net. But I kept going.

I flew over the fence.

I did a midair somersault.

I landed – *Wham!* – flat on my backpack.

Flat on Pop's lunch, I would find out later. Nan's thick, whole wheat sandwiches cushioned my fall and probably saved me from breaking my spine. But neither they nor the helmet stopped me from knocking myself nearly brainless.

I lay still for a few moments, blinking at the sky. My head hurt. Spots danced before my eyes, and I couldn't see right. The sun looked red. I moved my eyes painfully in their sockets and watched Susie scrambling to her feet on the other side of the fence. She didn't seem hurt. I still didn't fully understand what had happened.

Then I heard the sound of a two-stroke engine. The man on the motorcycle pulled up next to the fence and switched off the engine. He raised his visor and looked down at me through the sagging wires.

"What are you doing here, kid?" he asked.

"My horse got out of control," I gasped. I was winded, and it was hard to talk. "Who are you? What are you doing with Pop's bull?"

"Never mind," he snapped. He looked back across the paddock. "Was anyone with you?"

I wondered why he seemed angry with me. "No. I was taking Pop's lunch to him."

The man narrowed his piggy eyes at me. "Where's your pop now?"

"Up in the High Pasture," I said.

He nodded and seemed to think for a moment. "Okay," he said finally, as if reaching a decision. "Stay right where you are, kid, and I'll go get help."

He started the motorcycle and rode slowly along the fence line in Susie's direction. The little mare snorted and trotted out into the paddock, but the motorcycle followed her.

"Yaah! Yaah!" cried Pig-eyes, herding her in the direction of the black truck.

My heart thudded in alarm. Something weird was going on here. If he was going to get help, why was he taking Susie? And why couldn't *he* help me? He hadn't even asked if I was hurt. Grasping the fence, I dragged myself to my feet.

"Hey!" I called weakly. "Why are you taking my horse?"

Pig-eyes didn't slow down. I was still dazed, still winded, still badly shaken from my fall. My head throbbed. For more than a minute I simply stood there, supporting myself against the wobbly fence, watching helplessly as the motorcyclist herded Susie across the paddock. He chased her past the truck and out onto the road. Then he slapped her on the rump and watched her gallop away. The other man was closing the big doors at the rear of the truck when Pig-eyes rode back into the paddock. Kosciusko Rex was nowhere in sight.

Who were these men? Why were they on Nan and Pop's farm? What were they doing with Pop's prize Charolais bull?

Then it hit me. They were *stealing* him! They were the Jindabyne Rustlers!

3

COPPERHEAD SPUR

Nan and Pop had told me about the notorious gang of thieves that had been stealing cattle from farms all over the state. Known as the Jindabyne Rustlers, they had gotten away with more than a million dollars worth of livestock in the past eighteen months. The police had no idea who they were. There was a twenty thousand dollar reward for anyone who could provide information that would lead to their capture.

Twenty thousand dollars!

Peeling off my gloves and backpack, I half climbed, half rolled across the fence and set off at a slow, limping run towards the truck two hundred yards away. I knew there was no way I could stop the rustlers on my own, but I could get the truck's license plate number. The rest would be up to the police.

I was halfway across the paddock, too far away to read the license plate, when Pig-eyes swung his motorcycle in a wide semicircle and sped out onto the road. The truck followed.

I stopped running when I reached the gate. I was out of breath and dripping with sweat. A big chain and padlock lay coiled in the dust at my feet. The stainless steel hasp of the padlock had been cut cleanly in two. They were rustlers, all right.

I closed the gate. Pop's other bull, an old black rodeo bull called Chainsaw, was still in the paddock somewhere. Probably near the dam on the other side of the hill.

My head was throbbing, *thud, thud, thud.* After a few moments, I realized the thudding wasn't coming from inside my head.

"Susie!"

The little palomino came trotting back along the road. Pig-eyes had chased her away, but she'd come back for me. Forgetting my aches and bruises, I slipped through the gate and hobbled to meet her.

"Easy, Suze," I said.

Susie shook her head and snorted. The wasp sting in her ear was still troubling her. I stroked her flanks and continued talking softly. Then I put my left foot in the stirrup and cautiously swung up into the saddle. I had never done it on my own before. Susie stood there, as if I knew what I was doing. As if I was in control. I patted her neck.

"Good girl, Suze," I said.

I was faced with a dilemma. Which way should I go? Back to the farmhouse so that Nan could call the police? Or up to the High Pasture, which was closer, to let Pop know what had happened? Pop would have his cell phone with him, but the signal wasn't always reliable in this remote corner of the mountains, and he might not be able to get through to the police. He did have his four-wheel drive, however. We could go after the rustlers ourselves. But we might not be able to catch up to them. Pop wasn't a very fast driver, and the rustlers would have a thirty-minute head start.

There was a third possibility. I looked at the line of electricity transmission towers running up the side of Copperhead Spur. A rough path had been carved beneath them, through the forest, to give access to the tall metal towers and keep the wires clear of trees. According to Pop, it was a short cut to the Alpine Highway.

"If you're prepared to do a bit of mountain climbing," he'd joked a week earlier, as he and Nan drove me from the airport, "you could save yourself twenty miles by going over the spur instead of driving all the way around it."

I did a quick calculation. Nan and Pop's farm is high up in the mountains. The only way to it is Corcoran Road. It's an unpaved road that twists all the way to the outside world. There was no way a cattle truck with a bull on board could do more than thirty miles per hour along it. That gave me roughly forty minutes to cross the spur and meet the cattle thieves on the other side. I wasn't sure what I was going to do if I caught up with them. Probably I would get the truck's license plate number – and the motorcycle's, if it had one. First there was the problem of crossing Copperhead Spur, the long, craggy escarpment that towered over the farm and blocked out three quarters of the western sky.

"Susie," I said, "how good are you at climbing?"

④

AVALANCHE

Susie was pretty good at climbing. She needed to be. The electricity access trail was rough going. It was overgrown and incredibly steep. A hundred-foot-wide avenue slicing through the majestic old-growth forest, it went straight up the side of the spur.

For the first half a mile or so the going wasn't too bad. We zigzagged slowly upwards. Susie picked her way carefully through the knee-high bracken, skirting boulders and stumps and the rotting hulks of fallen trees. By leaning forward and taking most of my weight in the stirrups, like Nan had taught me, I managed to stay more or less in control – if you didn't count sliding off the back of the saddle a few times.

Then we came to a rockslide.

A thirty-foot-wide ribbon of scree and rocks and loose dirt, it looked unstable and dangerous. There was no way around it. Susie paused and turned her head, as if asking, *What now, boss?*

I didn't feel like anybody's boss. I glanced uncertainly upwards. We were only about five hundred feet from the skyline, but the gradient was nearly vertical. So near and yet so far. I wondered briefly about the strange, brownish cirrus clouds high overhead, then searched for another way up. The only alternative was to try the other side of the access trail. To get there we would have to skirt the nearest tower, which meant going back the way we had come for at least two hundred feet and losing precious altitude in the process. I looked at my watch. We had used up twenty minutes. There wasn't time for any more pussyfooting around.

"Giddy up!" I said, urging Susie forward.

Things began to go wrong as soon as the little mare stepped onto the rockslide. A stone rolled beneath one of her hooves, dislodging a small river of loose dirt and gravel. Susie fell awkwardly onto her haunches. She tried to stand up and fell again.

Her floundering hooves couldn't get a purchase in the rattling stream of gravel and stones and moving earth. She whinnied and began buckjumping desperately through the rockslide. It was too much for me. I couldn't hold on. Before I knew what had happened, I found myself dangling upside down, with my right foot caught in the stirrup. For a few terrifying moments I was dragged along, my helmet scraping and bumping over the gravel. Susie's sliding hooves came thumping down perilously close to my head. Then my foot popped out of the elastic-side boot I was wearing, and I was free. I rolled about fifteen feet and came to rest wedged against a tree stump. When I looked up, Susie was sliding down towards me, hindquarters first. She was going to crush me! At the last moment, she managed to dig in her hooves and halt her downward slide. A small avalanche of dirt and rocks continued on down and nearly buried me.

Coughing up grit, half blinded by dust, I dug myself out. A few yards away, almost directly above me, Susie was struggling to find traction on the near-vertical slope. Her hooves sank down to their fetlocks, but that didn't stop her kicking. Every kick showered me with rocks and dirt and swirling dust. Rolling out of the way, I scrambled on all fours up the slope and grabbed her bridle.

"Easy," I gasped. "Take it easy, Suze."

For a moment she quieted. Her eyes rolled back to look at me. I stroked her dirty, sweat-streaked face. "Okay, we can get out of this if we stay calm," I said, talking to myself as much as to Susie.

There was a rumbling sound. The ground trembled. I looked up and saw an extraordinary sight. Whole trees were moving! We had started a full-scale avalanche.

A boulder went thumping past so close that I felt the rush of air. More huge rocks rolled towards us. Susie let out a high-pitched scream. She reared, lost her balance, tipped slowly over and landed on her back, four legs flailing in the air. The ground shifted beneath her. A section of the mountainside was slipping down into the valley, taking Susie with it. The little mare began moving away from me, sliding down the slope on her back. I stood transfixed, my mind working in slow motion.

This is my fault, I realized. I had got her into this. If Susie died, the blame would rest squarely on my shoulders.

I launched myself across the sliding ground and managed to grab her reins. A tumbling rock hit me on the hip. Ignoring the pain, I leaned back against Susie's weight and dragged her around until gravity took hold and rolled her back onto her hooves. Nostrils flaring, eyes wide in fear, the terrified horse kicked and struggled to get a footing.

"Steady, Suze," I cried, ducking out of the way of another tumbling boulder. I held her reins firmly. Even though I was quivering inside, I tried to make my voice calm. "Follow me."

I led Susie at a right angle across the rumbling, shifting slope. It was hard to stay upright. My feet slipped and skidded. I'd lost a boot when I fell off Susie, and sharp stones bruised my foot through my sock. More boulders hurtled past. Tree stumps shook. Suddenly, a miniature crevasse opened at our feet. We leapt across it. And not a moment too soon. Where the crevasse had been seconds earlier, now there was a river of rocks and scree and tumbling boulders, as tons of unstoppable debris went crashing into the valley below.

Susie needed no further encouragement. Side by side, the little palomino and I scrambled for our lives.

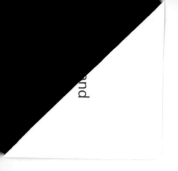

5

IN THE NICK OF TIME

Somehow we made it to solid ground. The mountainside below had stopped moving. A pall of dust hung in the air. Susie was trembling. Dirt and dust clung to her damp coat. She was a brown horse now. I patted her sweaty mane, and my hands turned brown too. She nickered softly and nuzzled my shoulder. It was a friendly gesture, but because of the steep gradient I nearly lost my balance.

"Hey, take it easy," I said, laughing for no reason. I guess I was just thankful to be alive.

I studied the skyline. The avalanche had carried us about fifty yards back down the slope. Now it was roughly six hundred feet to the top. It was a very steep climb. Could I manage it with one boot missing? I decided I could. By my reckoning, there were still eight or ten minutes left before the truck passed on the other side of the spur. It wasn't nearly enough time, but maybe I could get close enough to read the truck's license plate number. It was our only hope of getting Kosciusko Rex back.

I no longer thought of the twenty thousand dollar reward. It was Pop's pedigree bull that mattered. Nan reckoned he was worth as much as a house!

"Find your way home, Suze," I said, giving her a smack on the rump. It made me sad to watch her go down the side of Copperhead Spur towards the green strip of farmland far below, but the last section of the climb was too steep for a horse. I removed my helmet and hung it on a bush.

I won't be needing that any longer, I thought.

How wrong I was.

It took me three or four minutes to get to the top. It was a nearly vertical climb, and I was minus one boot. By the time I got to the top, I was exhausted, dripping with sweat and dying of thirst. It wasn't even midday, yet the temperature was soaring. It must have been well over a hundred degrees.

What a fool I'd been to leave the water bottle fastened to Susie's saddle! Limping because of my bruised foot, I crossed the narrow rocky pass and stopped in my tracks.

Shishkebab! Looming over the mountains, two or three miles to my left, was an enormous column of smoke. It hung over the shimmering landscape like a mushroom cloud from a nuclear explosion. Huge, motionless, menacing, it filled half the sky. I hadn't seen it earlier because Copperhead Spur had shielded it from view. The absence of wind meant that the column rose straight up for several thousand feet, until a slight movement in the upper atmosphere sent a faint, smoky haze in my direction. That explained the strange brown shadow that made the landscape dull and the eerie redness of the sun.

It was a bushfire, a big one. Alone at the top of Copperhead Spur, I watched the smoke, and my skin prickled. I knew there was no danger – it was too far away to pose a threat – but its sheer size was awesome. It would be pretty scary if it was closer – in the valley below, for instance. I wondered if there would be any way to escape it.

Corcoran Road traced a pale, wriggling path

through the forest far below. There was no sign of the truck yet. It was probably five or six minutes away.

Half a mile in five minutes, I thought, surveying the steep access trail that ran down this side of Copperhead Spur, too. It wasn't impossible. Competitors at the Olympics could run a mile in under four minutes. But I was no Olympian, and this was almost straight down. If I tried to run, there was a high possibility I would break my neck. Plus, I was wearing only one boot. I was never going to save Pop's bull.

"Sorry, Rex," I said, and looked around for a shady spot to rest and cool down.

I was about to make my way towards some Snow Gum trees when a flash of reflected sunlight caught my eye. Far to the right, the small, rectangular shape of the black truck came inching around a bend. The motorcycle was in front. It looked like a tiny speck. Moments later, both vehicles disappeared into another fold in the thickly forested foothills.

If only I could fly, I thought.

Leaves rustled behind me. I spun around, expecting to see a kangaroo or a wallaby. Instead, Susie trotted out of the trees. She'd followed me!

"Susie, you're a star," I gasped, surprised and pleased. "You got here in the nick of time."

6

OFF THE EDGE OF THE WORLD

The ride down the side of Copperhead Spur was crazy! If I'd had time to think about it, I would have chickened out. But the sight of the truck, and then Susie's unexpected arrival, somehow made me act without considering the risks.

For the first two hundred feet the drop was nearly vertical. It felt like we were jumping off the edge of the world. We went into free fall. I lay back against Susie's rump, gripping the saddle with my knees. My stomach was way up in my ribcage, and my eyes were scrunched tightly closed. Down, down, down we plummeted.

I felt a jarring thump. Then another. Then a

succession of thumps and a clatter of sliding rocks and flying hooves. I opened my eyes. Susie was still on her feet. Even more amazing, I was still on her back. But only just. My backside was taking a beating. My feet spiraled in the stirrups. My body and arms flopped out of control. I concentrated solely on staying in the saddle. There was nothing else below me, as far as I could see. Above me was a perfect view of the wide, smoky sky, interrupted every ten seconds when a towering electricity tower flashed by.

Somehow we made it. I don't know how long it took to get from the top of Copperhead Spur to the road. Enough time for my whole life to flash before my eyes. Fourteen years crammed into three thousand feet of free fall. I was dazed and giddy as I swung out of the saddle and planted my quaking feet on Corcoran Road.

It felt so-o-o-o-o good to have solid ground beneath me again.

So-o-o-o-o good to be alive.

Above us, a long curtain of drifting dust traced the path of our suicidal descent. I was shocked by the steepness. Did we really come down that? I patted Susie on her muddy, sweat-darkened shoulders. Both of us were trembling.

I hadn't forgotten our mission.

"What are we going to do about the truck, Suze?"
I asked.

Susie didn't answer. All I could hear was her loud,
blowing breath and the gurgle of a stream that flowed
under a rickety wooden bridge thirty feet away. The
little mare was pulling in that direction. She wanted a
drink.

"Go on," I said, releasing the reins. "You've
earned it."

There wasn't time for me to get a drink. I made
a decision. Taking the truck's license plate number
wasn't enough. I couldn't simply hide in the forest
and watch the cattle thieves drive by. Pop might
never lay eyes on his prize bull again if the truck
reached the highway. It was up to me to stop it.

While Susie picked her way down through
the rustling bracken to the stream, I limped onto
the bridge. It was a primitive construction: two
heavy wooden beams with a row of planks bolted
crosswise on top of them. There were no side rails.
I remembered crossing several of these bridges on
the way to the farm from the airport. The planks had

27

rattled noisily under the wheels of my grandparents' four-wheel drive. Sure enough, towards the middle of the bridge, I found a plank that had worked loose from one of the rusty bolts. By lifting one end and swinging it back and forth, I managed to free the other end as well. I slid the heavy plank off the edge of the bridge and dropped it into the stream.

Now there was a twelve-inch gap in the middle of the bridge. It wasn't wide enough – the truck might still get across. I tried the planks on either side of the gap. One was loose, but no matter how hard I pulled, I couldn't work it free of its bolts. Breathing heavily, I paused to wipe the sweat from my eyes.

That was when I heard it. Faint in the distance, hardly louder than the soft murmur of the stream, came the yammer of a two-stroke engine.

There wasn't much time. I made another attempt to rattle the loose plank from the bolts. No good. I couldn't work it free.

The sound of the motorcycle was unmistakable now. I glanced around. The gravel road curved away from me and disappeared behind a wall of towering gum trees about ninety yards from the bridge.

Think, I urged myself. *There's got to be a way.*

Then it came to me. I needed something to pry the plank loose. I looked around for a lever. Anything would do. It just needed to be long and sturdy enough to give me a slight mechanical advantage. *A fence post*, I thought, trying to block out the hum of the motorcycle, *or a good thick branch.*

A plank!

Seconds later, I was splashing like a madman through the stream. Susie raised her dripping muzzle from the water to watch me wade past in pursuit of the plank I'd tossed into the water. It was about fifteen feet downstream from the bridge. The plank was caught in some mossy rocks. Hefting it onto my shoulder, I crashed through the bracken and onto the end of the bridge.

The motorcycle sounded very close. Behind its high-pitched buzz came the low growl of the truck. They were just around the corner. I had ten seconds, maximum, before they swung into view and saw me.

Staggering out onto the bridge, I plunged the end of the dripping plank into the gap and leaned down with my full weight on the other end. Success! The second plank popped off its bolts as if they were made of play dough.

The sound of engines filled my ears. I tossed the first plank back into the stream and grabbed the second one. Not daring to look over my shoulder, afraid of what I'd see if I did look, I rushed to the edge of the bridge. And jumped.

7

DANGEROUS MEN

I missed the water. There hadn't been time to look where I was jumping. *Crunch!* I landed across the plank and might have broken several ribs had it not been for the heavy thicket of bracken that softened my landing. It really hurt. With a groan, I let go of the plank, rolled under the bridge and lay still.

The motorcycle skidded to a stop on the bridge. It was about three feet away, right over my head. I saw the knobbly tires through the slits between the planks, and the soles of Pig-eyes' boots. The noisy two-stroke engine went silent. From the road came the squeal of brakes. The truck's door creaked open.

"What's going on?" a man's voice asked.

"Dunno," said Pig-eyes. He had climbed off the motorcycle and was peering down through the gap in the bridge. Luckily, I was near the bank, where he couldn't see me. "Someone's messed with the bridge – taken out a couple of boards."

A second shadow fell across the planks, and the truck driver joined his mate at the hole. I could hear the engine idling gently in the background. "Vandals, d'you reckon?" he asked.

"Nah, not out here," said Pig-eyes. "Reckon someone wanted to stop us."

"Why?" asked the truck driver.

"Why do you think, Einstein? That's a pricey piece of livestock in the back of the truck."

"But ... but ... " stammered Einstein. "But nobody knows we've got it."

"There was that kid back at the farm. Isn't that his horse?"

Uh oh. I silently parted the bracken. Susie was standing three feet away, gazing in my direction.

Don't look at me! I wanted to shout at her. *You'll give the game away!*

Only this wasn't a game. These were cattle thieves, criminals. Dangerous men. Already Pig-eyes had tried to hurt me by forcing Susie into the fence. I should never have tampered with the bridge. Who knew what he and Einstein would do if they caught me now.

"It can't be the same horse," Einstein was saying. "We must have driven thirty miles."

"Maybe the kid knows a short cut. He told me he was Corcoran's grandson. He must know his way around."

"Wait till I get my hands on him," snarled Einstein.

"Forget it," Pig-eyes said. "He's probably hiding in the forest. We'll never find him." He lowered his voice. "But without a horse, the smart aleck will have a very long walk home."

I heard the clomp of boots. Then Pig-eyes vaulted down onto the creek bank and peered under the bridge. He was still wearing his crash helmet, but the visor was flipped open. For a moment it seemed like he was looking straight at me. I froze. My heartbeat was belting out a furious drum solo in my ears that blocked out everything else. I was all set to leap up and run. But I was in the shadows, partially screened by bracken, and Pig-eyes didn't see me. He walked off along the creek bank towards Susie.

"Here horsey," he said softly, raising his hand as if holding a lump of sugar. "Come to daddy."

Susie had no intention of letting him get anywhere near her. She probably remembered their last meeting. Shaking her head as if to say, *No way, José*, the little mare wheeled around and cantered off down the stream, splashing water in high silvery fans behind her. Pig-eyes chased her for five or six paces, then gave up.

"Forget the horse," Einstein called. "Let's fix this bridge and get out of here. I can see where the kid dropped one of the planks."

The next moment, the big truck driver came crunching down through the bracken on the other side of the bridge. He picked up the plank lying right next to me and hoisted one end up onto the bridge. I held my breath. If he looked down, he would see me. But Einstein was concentrating on fitting the plank into the gap in the bridge. He was looking up, not down.

I felt a sudden weight on my right hand, then a slow creeping movement. Lying flat on my belly in a bed of crushed bracken, my hand was only a few inches from my face. I swiveled my eyes down and nearly died of fright. I was eyeballing the biggest, ugliest, most horrendous-looking spider I had ever seen.

Its brown, furry body was the size of a mouse. Each of its eight, pinkish-brown legs was as long – and nearly as thick – as my little finger and covered in tufts of red and gray hair. It was almost as big as my hand. The worst part was its fangs. They were huge. Shiny black and viciously hooked, they looked like a pair of eagle's claws. They were so close to my face that I could see dewdrops of clear liquid glistening on their needle-sharp tips.

It was one of the bird-eating spiders that live in the region. Nobody knows how dangerous they are to humans, but they have been known to kill birds and animals as large as wallabies. The repulsive creature was sitting on my hand about four inches from my nose. I tried not to focus on the venom-dripping fangs. Two rows of beady black eyes returned my gaze.

I couldn't move. If I did, Einstein would see me. But I must have made a noise – a gasp or a groan – and attracted his attention. Suddenly a large hand closed like a vise around my other arm.

"Gotcha!" said the big cattle rustler.

DRIVING BLIND

There was only one thing to do. I flicked the hand with the spider on it upwards. Bull's-eye! The huge spider landed on Einstein's baseball cap. It was clinging onto the peak, dangling its heavy, egg-shaped body and at least four fat, pinwheeling legs right in front of Einstein's eyes. A shrill wail escaped his lips. He released my arm and straightened up, waving his hands like someone shooing away flies. But the spider wasn't going anywhere. Slowly, its weight pulled the cap forward and down on Einstein's head. Still waving his hands in useless circles, the big rustler took two blind steps backwards, lost his balance and fell backside-first into the creek.

I was out of there. Without a backward glance, I shot out on the other side of the bridge and scrambled up onto the road. Pig-eyes shouted something from further down the creek. I didn't hear what he said. I wasn't interested anyway. All I wanted to do was put as much distance as possible between myself and the two rustlers. My mind had closed down to everything else. *Get to the trees!* it was screaming. *Get to the trees and hide!*

I headed for the trees. It wasn't easy. I was wearing a boot on one foot, and a sock with holes in it on the other. The truck was standing in the middle of the road with its motor idling gently and the driver's door wide open. I was halfway past it when the little voice in my head stopped me in my tracks.

Whoa, boy! it said.

I did an about-face and dashed back to the front of the truck. Before I realized what I was doing, I swung up into the cab and slammed the door shut behind me.

I had never driven a truck before, but my brother Nathan had taught me to drive his Land Cruiser on some abandoned mining land back home in the Northern Territory. I didn't think this would be much different. I pressed the clutch in and pulled the long gearshift back into the "R" position. Ahead of me, Einstein lumbered up from under the bridge. He was no longer wearing the baseball cap, and his face was as white as a sheet. He didn't look very happy to see me in the truck.

I wasn't exactly delighted to see him, either. I put my foot on the accelerator and released the clutch. The engine stalled.

You forgot the handbrake, the little voice in my mind reminded me.

I was getting seriously worried. Einstein came pounding towards me, his face turning from white to red. There was murder in his eyes. Pig-eyes was clambering up out of the creek bed behind him. Quickly, I locked the driver's door, found neutral, and turned the key in the ignition. The engine rumbled back into life just as Einstein reached the truck. He grabbed the door handle and yanked. It was locked. He began banging on the window instead.

"Open up!" he shouted. "Unlock the door!"

Did he think I was an idiot?

Pig-eyes came running up on the other side. I leaned across quickly and locked the passenger door, too.

Now I had an angry rustler on each side of the truck, both banging on the glass and yelling blue murder. It was scary. If either of them got in, I would be in a lot of trouble. I was in a lot of trouble already. How was I ever going to get out of this? My hands were shaking so badly that I had difficulty releasing the handbrake. Then I clunked the gears into reverse, gave the engine plenty of gas and released the clutch.

The truck shot backwards with such force that Pig-eyes lost his grip and fell onto the road. I heard a rattle of hooves in the truck bed behind me and hoped Rex was okay. Pop's pride and joy would have to take care of himself for the next few minutes.

I was busy trying to keep us on the road. Nathan hadn't taught me how to drive in reverse. It was ten times harder than going forward, especially in such a big vehicle and with the road twisting and turning behind me. The truck veered crazily left and right, with Einstein swinging from the side mirror like an overweight acrobat. His face was as red as an overripe tomato. He was yelling at me to stop. Both of us knew I wasn't going to do that. I floored the accelerator, and finally he lost his nerve and let go.

Einstein hit the ground running. He kept running

for about a dozen paces, then slowed down to a stop and stood watching me, hands on hips, chest heaving. Behind him, Pig-eyes was charging back towards the bridge, where he'd left his motorcycle.

I tried to concentrate on driving. I wished I was going forward not backwards, but the road was too narrow to turn the truck around. To make matters worse, Einstein had bent the side mirror during his acrobat stunt, so I couldn't see behind me. I was driving blind. The truck weaved drunkenly from side to side, the engine roaring. I knew there was a bend coming up.

Almost too late, I remembered the passenger-side mirror. When I looked across, I saw a wall of trees rushing towards me. I slammed on the brakes and spun the steering wheel at the same time. The truck slewed sickeningly sideways. There was another clatter of hooves in the back and a thump that rocked the whole truck. Sorry, Rex!

The truck stalled. For a moment all I could see was swirling dust. When it cleared, I saw a stretch of straight road behind me in the passenger-side mirror. More through good luck than good driving, I had gotten the truck around the corner.

Einstein, Pig-eyes and the bridge were no longer in sight. I restarted the engine, slipped the gearshift back into reverse and stepped on the accelerator.

The next corner went the other way. It was a left-hand turn, and I had no mirror on that side. I had to open my door and hang out over the road to see where I was going. I was halfway around, crawling along at one mile per hour, when Pig-eyes and Einstein came screaming up on the motorcycle. Pig-eyes slid the machine to a dusty standstill. Einstein leapt off the back and rushed towards me. I just managed to close the door in time. The truck stalled. Einstein picked up a large rock from the side of the road and tried to smash my window. A web of spidery cracks spread across the glass.

"Unlock the door," he shouted angrily.

Terrified, unable to think straight, I turned the key and planted my foot. Einstein dropped his rock and jumped clear.

Somehow, I reversed the truck around the blind corner. A short section of straight road appeared in the rearview mirror. Sweat was dripping off me like rainwater. I wobbled the truck backwards along the narrow road. Driving in reverse is hard! And Rex wasn't making things easy for me. He was crashing around in the back, clattering his hooves and thumping the sides so hard that the truck rocked to and fro like a ship. And Pop reckoned his precious Charolais bull was as gentle as a lamb. Yeah, right!

The next corner was a right-hand turn – left, if you were reversing – and I got around it okay using the passenger-side mirror. I was wondering if it would be possible to drive all the way to Nan and Pop's in reverse, when Pig-eyes and Einstein caught up with me again. Pig-eyes rode the yammering motorcycle right up to the front of the truck. They were about three feet from the radiator grill, their heads poking above the truck's long black hood. Pig-eyes had a lot of dust on his visor, but I could see Einstein's face over his shoulder. If looks could kill, I would have been dead and buried at that moment.

Then Pig-eyes slammed on the brakes. Why was he stopping? I looked in the mirror.

Trees! My foot slammed down on the brake pedal. Too late.

There was a tremendous jolt, followed by a loud crash, then a series of bangs and scrapes and teeth-rattling vibrations. Finally, the truck thumped to a standstill, and a leafy branch fell across the windshield. Everything went silent and still. Except for a low, angry *"Moo"* in the compartment behind me.

⑨

MY PROBLEM NOW

Sweating in the hot, stuffy cab, I listened to the two men talking.

"That's the end of that," Pig-eyes said. "We'll never get it back on the road."

"What about the bull?" asked Einstein's deeper, slower voice.

"What *about* the bull? We can't very well plop him on the motorcycle, can we?"

"But the boss has been planning this one for months."

"Well, the boss messed up this time," Pig-eyes said angrily. "I told him we should have done this job at night. 'No, no,' he says, 'there'll be nobody on the farm all day Tuesday. Corcoran and his missus go bowling every Tuesday, regular as clockwork.' So what happens? We go on a Tuesday and run into a meddling kid on a horse!"

Now I understood why Pig-eyes had been surprised when I'd told him Pop was up in the High Pasture. They'd thought Nan and Pop were bowling. My grandparents hadn't gone bowling this week because I was staying with them. I had fouled up the rustlers' plans.

Einstein was thinking the same thing. "Just wait 'til I get my hands on the interfering little –"

"Forget the kid," Pig-eyes interrupted. "Let's get out of here while we still can. I don't like the look of that smoke."

I couldn't see any smoke from inside the truck. The leafy branch across the windshield obstructed my view. But I knew Pig-eyes was talking about the mushroom cloud I'd seen earlier. There wasn't any danger. If the cattle thieves had been up on Copperhead Spur, they would have seen that the fire was too far away to pose a threat. But I was happy to let them think otherwise. Anything to make them go away.

There was a crunch of feet as the two men walked past the truck's cabin. Einstein paused and turned. He thumped his big fist on the cracked glass of the side window.

"I hope it's a bushfire," Einstein said in a low, mean voice, "and I hope you fry!"

Moments later, the motorcycle howled into life and roared off into the distance.

I waited for two or three minutes, until I was absolutely sure the rustlers were gone. Then I unlocked the door and tried to open it. It was jammed. I had to crawl across and try the other door. There was a denim jacket on the passenger seat. It probably belonged to Einstein. I left it lying on the dirty floor and climbed out.

I was surrounded by trees. The truck had left the road and plowed backwards eighty feet into the forest, knocking over several small trees in the process. A branch lay across the top of the cab. The rear wheels were sunk up to their axles in a boggy creek bed. No wonder Pig-eyes and Einstein had given up. It would take another truck – or a bulldozer – to get it out.

Wondering how Kosciusko Rex had fared, I peered between the thick, wooden slats of the cattle pen on the back of the truck. A big red-rimmed eye glared out at me. There was an angry snort, and I got a face full of warm bull's breath. Then the eye disappeared. Next moment – *crunch!* – a massive horn punched clean through the wall of the truck, missing me by two inches. Wood splinters sprayed everywhere. I got such a fright that I lurched backwards, lost my balance and landed flat on my backside on the leaf-strewn ground.

Since when did Kosciusko Rex have horns? Pop's big white Charolais was a poley. He was meant to be hornless. Were there two bulls in the truck? I crept around to the other side and cautiously peeked through a gap low in the cattle pen. There was only one bull inside, and it wasn't Rex. It was a smaller, leaner animal. And it had a pair of heavy, flat-tipped horns as wide as the handlebars of a Harley Davidson. I would recognize those horns anywhere. So would hundreds of ex-rodeo riders all around the country. They belonged to Chainsaw, the meanest rodeo bull of all time. Now retired and living out the rest of his days on Nan and Pop's high-country farm.

The cattle rustlers had taken the wrong bull!

Peering into the truck, I realized what had happened. Chainsaw's hide was coated in dry white clay. He must have been rolling in boggy ground at the edge of the dam and changed from a black bull to a white bull. The rustlers had been ordered to steal a white bull and that's what they'd found. Instead of a champion Charolais stud bull with a pedigree five miles long, the idiots had stolen a mongrel rodeo outlaw that was famous, not for his breeding, but for his legendary bad temper. I had done them a favor by taking Chainsaw off their hands.

Now he was my problem.

RAINING FIRE

It took me four or five minutes to limp back to the bridge in my boot and sock. Susie was grazing quietly in the fuzz of grass growing beneath the bracken along the creek. I was relieved to see her. I'd been worried that Pig-eyes and Einstein might have caught her and taken her with them. Had they only known it, the palomino was worth more than the bull they'd just abandoned. But the rustlers had only stopped long enough to replace one of the planks so that they could get the motorcycle across the bridge. They had probably reached the Alpine Highway turnoff by now.

Provided the fire hadn't stopped them.

I didn't like the look of the smoke. Einstein's

parting words kept turning over in my mind. *I hope it's a bushfire, and I hope you fry!* A hot, midday wind had sprung up, pushing the smoke directly overhead. It covered the sky. I knew the fire was several miles away. The wind made it look worse than it was. Einstein's threat held no weight. I wasn't in any danger.

I took a long drink from the water bottle strapped to Susie's saddle and then mounted her. The mare seemed skittish. She pressed back her ears and tossed her head, snorting. When I urged her up the first low rise beneath the electricity tower, she shied sideways and tried to double back down to the road. I didn't blame her. We had already crossed Copperhead Spur once that day, and it hadn't been easy. But I needed to get back to my grandparents' farm as quickly as possible. Nan and Pop would be worried. And I wanted to tell them what had happened so that Pop could drive around in his own truck and fetch Chainsaw. It was turning into a stinking hot day, and the cranky old bull didn't have any water.

"Sorry, Suze," I said, pulling the nervous mare around and giving her a firm squeeze with my legs. "Whether you like it or not, we're going back over the spur."

Or so I thought. We only got halfway up. From there I had an unobstructed view over the ridge running parallel to Copperhead Spur. What I saw was frightening. The fire looked a lot closer than I had thought. The wall of smoke seemed to be rising out of the next valley, a little less than half a mile away. That was impossible! An hour or so earlier it had been two or three miles distant. A fire couldn't move that fast.

Then I noticed the wind. Earlier, the day had been hot and still. Now a gusting northerly blew in my face, bringing with it the acrid smell of burning eucalyptus. Susie smelled it too. She stamped her hooves and nickered softly. I held her steady. Even though it was early afternoon, an eerie darkness had fallen over the mountains. The sun was a dim red disk, barely visible through the tide of thick smoke that swept across the sky.

I watched a black ember float down on the wind towards us, trailing a thin ribbon of blue smoke. Soft as a feather, it landed on a dry frond of bracken not ten feet from where I sat on Susie's back. The frond smoked for a moment, then arched its back and blossomed into a flaming yellow flower. I slid down from the saddle and stamped the flame out with my boot. Before I could remount, another ember floated down fifty feet away. I hurried over to stamp it out, too. When I turned around, I saw another. And another. All around, faster than I could get to them and stamp them out, glowing embers were falling from the sky in a silent red shower.

It was raining fire.

Then I saw something even more frightening. On the skyline several hundred feet above, a bright snake of flame slithered up the trunk of a gum tree. It coiled swiftly through the branches, then the whole treetop burst alight.

A spot fire had started on Copperhead Spur!

For several moments, I couldn't move. I stood in the knee-high bracken, watching as my escape route was cut off by the new fire. A flock of black cockatoos swooped overhead, their raucous cries shaking me from my trance. I swung back into the saddle.

"Let's get out of here, Susie."

With a prod of my heels, I sent the little mare charging back down into the valley.

11

WILL·O'·THE·WISPS

A mob of about thirty kangaroos came thumping along Corcoran Road as we reached it. Spooked by the smell of smoke, they hardly paid any attention to us, whizzing past us on both sides. They were so close that one actually brushed my right stirrup. A couple of the big bucks bounced nearly as high as me. Susie wanted to race them, but I held her back. The kangaroos went bounding into the distance. I wished them good luck. If anything could outrun a bushfire, I reckoned a kangaroo could.

I wasn't so sure about a bull, though. Leaving Susie on the road, I limped down to the truck and jumped the boggy creek bed. There was a big door on the back of the truck that swung down and acted as a ramp. It had landed on a clump of ferns, leaving a half-yard drop at the end. The ferns were like a springy mattress underneath it. When I tried pushing down on the ramp, it bounced right back up again. Chainsaw came clopping to the open doorway and gave me a mean glare. I backed away quickly.

"Come on, big guy," I called to him, ready to run if I had to.

Chainsaw put one large hoof on the half-lowered ramp, then paused when it wobbled. If he came one step further, his weight would push it all the way down. But the bull shook his massive head, as if to say, *No way am I walking down there*, and reversed back into the truck.

The rustlers' rope was still tied around Chainsaw's neck. It trailed between his front legs and disappeared back into the truck. Using a long stick, I managed to hook its end and pull it out. The rope was nice and long, about eight or nine yards. This suited me fine – I wanted as much distance as possible between him and me. But he wouldn't cooperate. No matter how hard I pulled, Chainsaw wouldn't leave the safety of the truck bed. The bouncy ramp made him nervous.

Time to put Plan B into action. Recrossing the creek bed, I tried coaxing Chainsaw out next to the ramp, rather than down it. From here, it was a small drop into the ferns. The ground was soft, and he wouldn't hurt himself.

"C'mon, *jump*," I encouraged him, pulling hard on the rope. "I know you can do it. I've seen Pop's videos."

In one of them, Chainsaw jumped so high that the unfortunate cowboy on his back nearly went into orbit. They carried the man away on a stretcher, which was what happened to a lot of the hopefuls that tried to ride Chainsaw. How times change. Now the grand old warrior of the rodeo circuit was nineteen years old. He had retired from the rodeo scene, and it looked as if he had retired from jumping as well.

Maybe he needs someone on his back to get him moving, the little voice in my head suggested.

That is so not going to happen! I told it.

In Chainsaw's long and illustrious career, no one had ever stayed on his back the full eight seconds to the bell. Four hundred and twelve men had tried, four hundred and twelve men had bitten the dust. No way in the world was I going to be number four hundred and thirteen.

I dropped the rope and retrieved the stick. Walking around the side of the truck, I poked it in through one of the gaps and prodded Chainsaw in the rump. There was a thunderous clatter of hooves, then the stick jerked in my hand. I pulled it back out and discovered I was only holding half a stick. A long, flat-tipped horn waved menacingly through the gap.

"I'm trying to *help*," I cried in frustration.

Einstein's words came back to me, and I asked, "You don't want to be barbecued, do you, Chainsaw?"

I know *I* certainly didn't. How far away was the fire? The hot, northerly wind was growing stronger. With it came the unmistakable smell of smoke. A faint blue haze drifted through the trees.

Back on the road, Susie suddenly raised her head. A wallaby darted past, but the mare paid no attention. She was intent on something else, further up the road. Her nostrils flared, her ears poked forward. I listened too. What was that drumming sound?

Hooves. Galloping hooves.

With a great thundering rush, a herd of horses flew by. There were about a dozen of them. A motley collection of browns, grays, brindles and pintos. Brumbies! Nan had told me there was a herd of the legendary wild horses still living in the mountains. For years, she and Pop had wanted to catch and tame them. They didn't stand a chance. Brumbies are too elusive. Will-o'-the wisps, Nan called them. Today, the bushfire had flushed them out.

"Susie," I yelled, charging through the trees. "Come back!"

Nan's little mare was running after the brumbies. By the time I reached the road, she was galloping behind them, reins and stirrups flying. I shouted again. It was no use. The wild horses' panic had infected her. All I could do was stand and watch as Susie and the brumbies faded into the drifting blue smoke like will-o'-the-wisps.

ONE WAY OUT

After Susie and the wild brumbies had gone, I became aware of a hot, throbbing sensation in my foot. I looked down.

At first I could not fully grasp what my eyes were telling me. Red paint. Why was I standing in a puddle of red paint?

That isn't paint, the little voice in my head informed me. *That's ...*

I didn't pass out – I simply sat down very quickly in the middle of the dirt road.

... blood.

It was my right foot – the one without a boot. Very carefully, I peeled off the remains of the sock.

There wasn't much of it left, just a ragged flap of filthy, wet wool. My foot was a mess. There was blood all over it, with a thick layer of dirt stuck to that. I dabbed gingerly at the underside with the ruined sock, cleaning the gunk away. The blood was coming from a deep gash in my heel, oozing out like runny tomato sauce. This time I very nearly did pass out.

Pull yourself together, the little voice in my head commanded. *There's a bushfire coming. If you don't act quickly, you'll wind up barbecued.*

I needed something to tie around my foot so that I could walk on it. Something to stop the flow of blood. A bandage of some kind. I looked at the sock. It was useless, but it gave me an idea. Wrenching the boot off my left foot, I whipped off the good sock and wrapped it twice around my right heel. Then I tied the ends together on top of my foot like a fat shoelace. It didn't work. The weave of the wool was too loose, and the blood started soaking through almost immediately.

I was beginning to tremble. Shock was setting in. It was hard to think clearly. Hard to concentrate on anything but my rising panic. I was going to die. The fire was going to get me. Or I'd bleed to death. Either way, I was history.

Then I remembered Pop's shirt. Even though it was summer, Nan had insisted I wear one of Pop's long-sleeved farmer's shirts. "To keep the sun off," she reckoned. The sun was the least of my problems now. It had all but disappeared behind the mass of thick smoke that rolled overhead like thunderclouds, transforming the early afternoon into an eerie brown twilight.

With fumbling fingers I unbuttoned the shirt. *Sorry, Pop*, I thought, biting through the hem on one shoulder and ripping out the sleeve. I tied it around my foot. It seemed to stop the blood.

I put the ripped shirt and my boot back on. Then I stood up and gingerly tested my foot. It hurt when I put my heel down, but I could walk on my toes without too much pain. I limped down the slope towards the truck. A short distance from the road, I passed the splintered stump of a small sapling. The truck had sheared it off at ground level, leaving several tall spikes of wood sticking up like long, narrow teeth. One of the spikes glistened wetly with blood. I gave it a wide berth. I couldn't afford any more accidents. Now that Susie had run off and I could hardly walk, there was only one way out of this mess.

I had to ride Chainsaw.

1,2,3 ...

Bulls are color blind, so it doesn't matter what color rag you wave at them. Blue is just as good as red. It's the waving that makes them mad.

"Yaaah! Yaaah! Yaaah!" I yelled, jiggling Einstein's blue denim jacket in Chainsaw's face. "Chase it, you big wuss!"

I'm not actually as brave – or as stupid – as that makes me sound. I wasn't in front of Chainsaw while I jiggled the jacket in his face. The jacket was dangling from the end of a long stick, and I was standing off to one side of the ramp. If Chainsaw went for me, I could dive under the truck. I hoped that wouldn't happen. My plan was to make him mad enough to chase the jacket down the ramp. After that, I hoped he and I could settle our differences. My life depended on it. Because of my injured foot, Chainsaw was my ticket out of there. I couldn't make it on my own.

First I had to get the stubborn old bull out of the truck. But he wasn't cooperating.

"Chainsaw, come *on!*" I yelled in frustration.

Time was running out. Although I couldn't see the fire, I could hear it: a distant, low roar, like the ocean breaking on a rocky coastline. The wind was scorching hot and filled with smoke and ash and falling cinders. Flocks of birds flew screeching overhead. Another wallaby went crashing through the ferns behind me.

"*Yaaah! Yaaah! Yaaah!*" I flopped the jacket so close to the bull that it snagged on one of his big, blunt horns.

That got a reaction. Chainsaw jerked his nose skyward, dragging the jacket off the end of the stick. It fell across his eyes. The bull snorted and shook his head from side to side, but the jacket was caught on his horns, and he couldn't dislodge it. Bellowing with rage, Chainsaw swung blindly around and slammed into the side of the truck with such force that the vehicle rocked on its springs. Wood splinters scattered all around me. I fell backwards into a clump of ferns. Lying on the ground, I could no longer see into the truck. But I could see Chainsaw. His big, ugly head, now without its blue denim hood, stood out against the smoky sky almost directly above me. He had punched his head right through the side of the truck!

Chainsaw rolled one big eye down to look at me. Snot dangled from his nose. His breathing was heavy. From inside the truck came the clatter and scrape of hooves, as the bull tried to drag his head back through the hole. One of the broken slats poked out slightly, and its splintered end jabbed into Chainsaw's neck like the barb of a fish hook. The more he pulled backwards, the more it dug in. He was stuck.

I couldn't get close enough to free Chainsaw from the headlock he'd gotten himself into. Every time I reached to grab the broken slat, he went totally nuts, bellowing and stamping and thrashing his head around like a hooked barramundi. The whole truck creaked and shook. After two or three attempts, I gave up. There were flecks of blood on Chainsaw's neck where the wooden barb was digging into him. He was going to kill himself.

"Settle down, big guy," I said, using my remaining

sleeve to wipe a mixture of sweat and drool off my forehead. "You're just making it worse for yourself."

Worse for both of us. A small spot fire had started in a clump of ferns fifty yards along the creek. It was only a matter of minutes before the flames reached the truck. I would have to make a run for it. Now that I'd seen how psycho Chainsaw was, I knew I could never ride him. If all those professional rodeo riders couldn't ride him, what chance did I have? I was only a boy, with no rodeo experience. I hadn't even ridden a horse until five days ago. If I was going to escape the bushfire, I would have to make it on my own, regardless of my injured foot. I couldn't outrun the flames, but I might be able find some place to give me shelter. A cave perhaps. Or I could lie in the creek and use a reed like a snorkel to breathe through while the fire front swept over me. I hobbled down to have a look. At this point, the creek wasn't deep enough, but if I followed it downstream …

I looked back over my shoulder. Chainsaw's ugly head poked out of the truck's side like a hunter's trophy on a wall. I couldn't leave him there. He would be totally helpless when the fire came. I had to get him out.

Swinging myself clumsily up onto the ramp, I limped into the cattle pen. Chainsaw heard me behind him and renewed his efforts to get free. His big hooves knocked and slid on the wooden floor. He let out another loud, angry bellow.

"Chill out!" I cried, keeping clear of his flailing hooves. "I'm trying to help you."

Chainsaw seemed to fill the whole truck. He might have been smaller than Kosciusko Rex, but up close he looked massive. Did I really want to do this? With nowhere to retreat to in the back of the truck, I could end up squashed like a bug on a windshield.

Using the slats as ladder rungs, I clambered awkwardly up the truck's side. It was easy to squash the toes of my bandaged foot into the narrow gaps, but the boot on my left foot kept slipping. I had to concentrate or I'd fall. Once I was high enough, I worked myself along until I was directly above the struggling animal. It was a frightening view. Chainsaw looked like a dinosaur. The white clay had rubbed off in places, exposing patches of scarred, leathery hide speckled with thick black bristles. I inched my way down until my legs straddled his massive shoulders without actually touching him. Sweat dribbled into my eyes. My heart was quaking right off the Richter scale. Carefully placing the sole of my boot against the wooden barb that pressed into Chainsaw's neck, I pushed with all my might.

Three things happened almost simultaneously:

The wood broke.

Chainsaw dragged his head out of the hole.

I slipped and fell.

(14)

CRASH TEST DUMMY

I hadn't meant to ride Chainsaw. My plan was to free him from the headlock he'd got himself into, then clamber out over the side of the truck. I was sure the old bull would figure out how to go down the ramp when the fire got close enough. But when I found myself sitting on Chainsaw's neck, with my hands gripping his huge handlebar horns, I had no choice but to hang on and hope for the best.

Riding Susie with a wasp in her ear was a walk in the park compared to this. It was like being caught in a tornado. Around and around we went, bucking, twisting, jolting, crashing into the truck's sides, spinning, spinning, spinning … flying. Yes, flying.

I'd lost my grip on Chainsaw's horns. My feet went cartwheeling across the smoky sky above me. I saw a blur of trees, ferns, the ramp, then one of Chainsaw's huge hooves coming down like a battering ram.

Crunch!

The pain was like an explosion in my left foot. I nearly blacked out. But I fought to stay conscious, knowing my life depended on it. I rolled out of the way as Chainsaw thundered past down the ramp. Biting back a howl of agony, I stood up. My left foot was killing me. I couldn't put any weight on it. But I'd worry about that later. Right now my only concern was Chainsaw. If he came after me I was history.

Balancing on the toes of my right foot, I turned to see where he was. I sighed with relief. The old bull was headed in the opposite direction, trailing the rope behind him as he trotted off along the creek into the blue smoke.

"Don't come back!" I called after him. Then I collapsed onto the ramp to take a look at my foot.

The pain was a deep, throbbing ache. My boot felt tight, as if I'd suddenly outgrown it. Gingerly, I eased the boot off. It was so painful I nearly blacked out again. Already the bridge of my foot was turning red and purple. It was visibly swollen. I didn't need an x-ray to know it was broken.

I tossed the useless boot into the ferns beside the ramp. One foot spiked, the other one broken. *I'm finished*, I thought.

Something beeped inside my head.

And now I was hearing things. I watched a scruffy brown wombat go lolloping past without giving me so much as a sideways glance. Two crimson parrots flew screeching through the smoke. The fire was very close. I should have been trying to get away, like the wombat and the parrots, but I couldn't walk. What was I going to *do*?

I heard the beeping noise again. It was barely audible above the muffled roar of the approaching fire. Slowly, I turned my head. The sound seemed to be coming from the truck, inside the cattle pen.

Beep-beep-beep. Beep-beep-beep.

A cell phone? I crawled up the ramp on my hands and knees. A pile of denim lay in the middle of the filthy floor. It was Einstein's jacket, and it was ringing.

The phone was in one of the pockets. It was tiny and hardly weighed anything. No wonder I hadn't noticed it earlier. Chainsaw must have stood on it, or crushed it against the wall of the truck when he had the jacket on his head. The LCD screen was broken, the keypad had fallen off. Yet the tiny phone still worked! It trilled and vibrated in my hand like an oversized cricket. I pressed a fingernail into the recess where the talk button should have been.

"Adam, did you get it?" a man's voice said faintly in my ear.

My first inclination was to tell the caller who I was and to send a helicopter to rescue me. Then I realized who I was talking to. Adam must be Einstein's real name, and this was one of his friends. He wasn't likely to help me.

"Adam, are you there?" the caller asked.

It's hard to explain why I impersonated Einstein. I guess I couldn't accept that my number was up. Things certainly looked bad but, in the back of my mind, I knew there must be a way to get out of this mess. And when I escaped, I was going to bring the Jindabyne Rustlers to justice.

"Yes, it's me," I said, making my voice deep.

"Did you get it?"

"Are you talking about the bull?" I asked.

"Of course I'm talking about the bull. Did you get it?"

"Yeah, we got it, no worries."

"Why haven't you called?" the man asked. "Mr. Cameron's getting jittery."

I had to think quickly. The caller was obviously another member of the Jindabyne Rustlers gang. Mr. Cameron must be their boss. If I went on pretending to be Adam, I could find out more about them. "There wasn't any signal in the mountains," I said, in my Einstein voice. "Where are you calling from?"

"Blue Horizon Downs. I've been here for nearly an hour. Mr. Cameron wants to know when you'll get here."

Blue Horizon Downs. It sounded like the name of a farm. "We should be there soon," I said.

There was a pause. "You sound strange," the man said.

I spoke through my cupped hand and left gaps in what I was saying, as if the signal was dropping out.

"Yeah, you're breaking up … too. Need … tell you … important. Give me … Cameron's landline number … call you … from phone booth."

I heard voices in the background. Then the man came back on the phone and gave me Mr. Cameron's number. It was easy to remember because it ended in three fours.

Gotcha! I thought, and ended the call.

Now I had two names – three, if you counted Pig-eye – as well as the name of a farm and a phone number. All I had to do was give the information to the police, and I'd be twenty thousand dollars richer!

But all the money in the world wasn't going to help me escape the bushfire. Einstein's phone had no keypad, so I couldn't dial out. I tossed it aside and picked up the denim jacket. A blast of boiling wind swirled into the truck. It seemed ridiculous to be putting on a jacket when it was so hot, but in a bushfire you're supposed to wear heavy clothes. I buttoned it up to the collar.

I was hopping to the ramp when Einstein's phone started beeping again. I glanced back where I'd dropped it. It was probably just his friend again. I was in a hurry – the fire sounded *close* – but what if it was someone else? What if it was someone who could help me? I hopped back towards the beeping phone.

And that's what saved my life.

There was a loud *whoosh*, a gust of hot air on my back, and suddenly the truck's interior lit up as bright as the beach on a sunny day. My shadow rushed to meet me as I tumbled forward like a crash test dummy. I hit the floor hard and crawled on my belly to the front of the cattle pen. Behind me, a wall of yellow flame completely filled the doorway.

The fire front had arrived. I was trapped!

SELF-PRESERVATION IS
A POWERFUL INSTINCT

I cowered against the metal wall at the front of the cattle pen, as far away from the leaping flames as possible. It wasn't far enough. The unprotected skin on my face and hands stung from the fierce heat. My eyeballs felt scorched. There was no air. The breath was being sucked from my lungs as if by a giant vacuum cleaner. I was suffocating.

Beside me on the filthy floor, the phone was still beeping. I didn't care who was on the other end. I grabbed it and jabbed a fingernail into the hole where the talk button used to be.

"Help me!" I gasped. "My name is Sam Fox and I'm trapped in a truck near Copperhead Spur. There's a bushfire all around me!"

For a few seconds there was nothing. Just the whisper and crackle of flames. Then I heard a familiar deep voice in my ear.

"Tough luck, kid. You shouldn't have stuck your nose in where it wasn't wanted."

It was Einstein, or Adam, as I knew him now. He and Pig-eyes must have made it safely to Mr. Cameron's and figured out that I had his phone.

I was gasping for air. It was almost impossible to talk. "Can't you help me?" I whispered.

"How am I supposed to help you?"

"Call the police," I wheezed, then realized how ridiculous my request was. As if the rustler was going to call the police!

"Call them yourself," Adam said, and hung up.

I let the phone slip from my fingers. *I will call the police*, I promised. *And when I do, they'll come looking for you.*

My breath came in big, rasping sobs. The oxygen in the air was being consumed by the fire. I was growing dizzy and disoriented from carbon monoxide poisoning. It was hard to think clearly. I was trapped. The rear of the truck was completely alight now. Sheets of yellow flame leapt up the wooden sides and sailed off into the smoke-filled sky. I watched the sky for a moment, then my oxygen-starved brain kicked in, and I realized I wasn't trapped. The top of the truck was open. I could climb out.

It was like being in a strange, slow-motion dream. My mind seemed to shut out the terrible heat, the pain in my broken foot, the lack of oxygen. I scrambled to my feet, taking my weight on my hands and the toes of my right foot. The air quivered. I knew I couldn't breathe in – the burning air would sear my throat and lungs. So I kept my mouth firmly shut. I ordered myself not to breathe in through my nose, either. My chest quivered. My vision became dark and misty.

I faced the wall in the front corner of the cattle pen. I put my fingers between the slats. I began climbing.

When I reached the top, I looked down on the dusty black roof of the truck's cab. The fallen branch still lay across it, but at least it wasn't burning. There were no flames between me and the road. Just a thick soup of flying sparks and cinders and swirling blue smoke. Behind me, the rear half of the truck was completely enveloped by fire. The nearest flames were only two or three yards away. The wind whipped them around like deadly yellow snakes. The heat was intense.

I rolled over the edge and fell through the leaves onto the roof of the cab. I landed on my right hip and shoulder. My ears no longer seemed to be working. I gulped air. It was full of smoke, but at least there was oxygen in it. I filled my starved lungs. For four or five seconds I lay on the roof of the cab, gasping like a newly landed fish, letting the oxygen replace the poison in my blood. There was a whistling sound in my ears, and my hearing returned. I could smell singed hair. My left foot was throbbing. My right foot felt sticky with blood. I was hurting all over, but at least I was alive. The fire was behind the truck, not in front of it. It was just the spot fire I'd seen earlier! The wind must have driven it along the creek and made it larger. The main fire wasn't here yet. There was still a chance I could escape.

I pushed myself to the edge of the cab and swung down to the ground, using the bent mirror for support. I was careful not to put any weight on my broken left foot. My right foot was okay as long as I kept the bandaged heel off the ground. I started hopping through the trees. The burning truck roared and crackled behind me. My eyes stung. I felt weak and bruised and light-headed, but self-preservation is a powerful instinct. I had to escape the fire. I wasn't going to let it beat me.

I got as far as the road, then collapsed in an exhausted heap.

TOO SLOW

I had to think fast. What would my brother Nathan do in a situation like this?

Nathan is a tour guide in the Northern Territory. He's a survival expert. *Make your surroundings work for you*, he told me once. *The forest is your friend, not your enemy.*

Today it was my enemy. It was bringing the fire. If I remained in the forest, I was going to die. So much for Nathan's words of wisdom.

There was a rustling noise behind me. I sat up and watched a three-foot-long goanna scurrying along the edge of the road. It was followed by a small furry animal – a bush rat or a bandicoot. From further up among the trees came the *thump thump thump* of fleeing wallabies and kangaroos. Overhead, the sky was dotted with birds and bats and winged insects. Everything was going in same direction: away from the fire.

They had the right idea.

I struggled to my feet – to my *foot*, actually – and started hopping down the middle of the road, following the fleeing wildlife. I had gone less than twenty yards when I had to sit down and rest. It was hopeless. No way in the world could I make it on my own. Not on one foot. Certainly not on the *toes* of one foot. The fire would overtake me within a few hundred yards, provided I didn't drop dead from exhaustion first. *Either way I was probably going to die*, I thought, as I watched an echidna pass me and go waddling down the road.

Why hadn't I tied Susie to a tree? It was because I hadn't stayed calm. Because I hadn't been *thinking*. If I wanted to stay alive, I had to use my head. I had to think my way out. Nathan's words came back to me: *Make your surroundings work for you*.

I stood up and looked around. Trees, bushes, ferns, rocks, fallen branches ...

Fallen branches!

I found two branches with forked ends. One was too long, so I inserted it in the narrow gap between two saplings and twisted it sideways until it snapped. I tested it again. Now it was slightly too short, but it was better than nothing. I had a pair of crutches.

They worked. I hobbled along at a reasonable pace for about a hundred yards. I even passed the echidna. But I wasn't going fast enough. I could hear the growing roar and crackle of the fire behind me. I could feel the hot wind like dragon's breath on my back. The pungent smoke burned my nostrils and stung my eyes. It was so thick that I could barely see ten yards ahead.

Then I heard another sound. A drumming noise. I stopped in the middle of the road. The noise grew louder. Suddenly a large, indistinct shape materialized out of the smoke ahead. Susie! My heart pumped with relief. Nan's little palomino had come back for me.

I was wrong. The shape didn't turn into a galloping horse. It was a bull. Charging straight at me. At about a sixty miles per hour.

NUMBER 413

Time stood still.

In the second or two before Chainsaw hit me, my brain went into overdrive. It told me that Chainsaw was going the wrong way. He was running towards the fire, not away from it. My brain also noted that Chainsaw's head was raised. If he'd been charging, his head would be lowered. And he looked confused, not angry.

Make your surroundings work for you, I remembered.

Chainsaw didn't see me until the last moment. He swerved to one side, struck me a glancing blow and thundered past. I spun in a circle. My crutches went flying. As I toppled to the road, one of Chainsaw's sledgehammer hooves missed my head by inches.

I barely noticed the close call. Dragging past me through the dust was a long piece of rope. I made a desperate lunge for it.

Here's what my brain had worked out as Chainsaw charged towards me: the old bull was panicked and disoriented. He didn't know which way to go. *I* knew which way to go, but I could barely walk. Together, with my brain and Chainsaw's brawn, we might be able to escape the bushfire.

It was a good plan, but the reality was daunting. I would have to succeed where four hundred and twelve professional rodeo riders had failed. I would have to ride Chainsaw.

First I had to *stop* him. I grabbed the rope and held on grimly. The other end was tied around the galloping bull's neck. Chainsaw weighed a ton. I weighed one hundred and thirty pounds. It was no contest.

Dragging along the road a couple of yards behind Chainsaw's swaying rump, I wasn't slowing him down at all. His big, plate-sized hooves flashed in my face. I was eating his dust, literally. Soon my eyes were so full of grit that I had to close them. My front burned from friction with the road. It grew hotter and hotter as my borrowed clothes – Adam's jacket, Pop's trousers – became thin and shredded. Soon it would be just my bare skin versus the gravel road. *Definitely* no contest. I let go.

I rolled a couple of times, then lay still. Not for long. I could still feel heat, but this was a different kind of heat. A great crackling roar filled my ears. When I raised my head, I saw a terrifying sight. A wall of flames towered above the treetops ahead. It must have been a hundred and fifty feet high and seemed to be rushing towards me. The heat was unbelievable. When I stood up, it nearly bowled me over.

Chainsaw was ten yards further up the road, ten yards closer to the fire front. He stood motionless, watching the approaching flames. Then he turned his head and looked at me. His eyes were red and half closed. Big tears dribbled down from them. It dawned on me what was wrong with him. He was nearly smoke-blind. No wonder he seemed so lost and confused. I hopped towards him, talking soothingly as I approached. Chainsaw allowed me to come right up to him and pat his heaving flank.

So far, so good. Ignoring the heat and the din of

the approaching firestorm, I took a firm hold of the loop of rope tied around Chainsaw's tree trunk neck. Although he was the size of a car, he wasn't as tall as Susie. Problem was, he had no saddle and no stirrups. *This is lunacy*, I thought. But it was my only option.

"Okay, old fella, don't freak out on me," I said nervously.

I hauled myself clumsily onto Chainsaw's back.

There was no reaction. He simply stood there as I pivoted my body around and sat up in a riding position, my legs splayed wide like a mahout on an elephant. I held the rope collar firmly in both hands.

"Giddy up!" I said.

Chainsaw didn't move. I had been sitting on him for about ten seconds. That's longer than any rider in history. But, as far as I was concerned, those were ten wasted seconds. Time was precious. The fire front was about a hundred yards away. I saw a tree literally explode, sending a rain of flaming branches and burning bark in all directions.

"C'mon Chainsaw, get moving!"

I kicked his ribs. That only hurt my sore feet. Chainsaw stood still. He had never been ridden before, except in a rodeo arena, and he didn't know what I wanted. I turned the collar of Einstein's jacket up against the terrible heat of the approaching flames. The heat was bothering Chainsaw too, but not as much as the smoke. His eyes were running like leaking faucets. He flicked an ear, then shook his head vigorously from side to side, trying to clear his vision.

"It's fire, Chainsaw," I cried. "You've got *to run away* from it!"

He was nineteen years old. For a bull, that's about a hundred, so it isn't surprising that he was confused by everything that was going on.

The firestorm was descending on us like a flaming tsunami. There was no time to hang around. Dragging at Chainsaw's rope collar, I pulled it around until I could reach the knot. Then I tugged the rope's loose end up and coiled it on the bull's withers until just a yard was left. With one hand gripping the rope collar, I swung the loose end like a whip in my other hand and whacked Chainsaw on the rump. It worked. He began walking slowly away from the fire. Walking, not running.

The fire was only fifty yards away. It roared as loud as a jumbo jet. The air rippled and quivered with heat.

And Chainsaw was *walking!*

"Get a move on!" I yelled, whacking him again.

He didn't speed up. Crazy old bull. Didn't he realize we'd be cooked in about thirty seconds?

Part of the fire had already caught up with us. Not far to our left was the black silhouette of the fiercely burning truck.

I should never have tried to save Chainsaw, I thought bitterly. I should have stayed on Susie and looked after myself. Now, because of a senile old bull who didn't even have the sense to run away from a bushfire, I was going to …

Boom!

TRAVELING ZOO

According to Pop, there was only one thing that Chainsaw feared: fireworks.

Some idiot had thrown a firecracker into his trailer at a rodeo once. Chainsaw went psycho. He completely demolished the trailer, then totaled two parked cars and a camper.

If I ever meet the person who threw the firecracker, I would like to shake his hand. Because to a bull that's afraid of fireworks, an exploding truck must seem like the mother of all firecrackers.

The blast from the truck's detonating fuel tank nearly blew me off Chainsaw's back. Luckily, I was able to hold on, because the next thing I knew the old bull was running for his life. For both our lives. Away from the exploding truck and away from the firestorm.

It was a wild, bumpy, terrifying ride. Doubly terrifying, because I knew that to fall off Chainsaw's back would be fatal. He wasn't going to stop for me, or for anything. It was every man and bull for himself. I twisted both hands through his rope collar and held on.

Pretty soon we began passing animals. The echidna. A koala. Lizards, snakes, possums, centipedes, wombats, lyrebirds. Even a spotted quoll. It was like a traveling zoo. This time all of us were going the same way. There was only thing on our minds: survival.

A small yellow and green bird, some kind of honeyeater, landed on Chainsaw's neck and hitched a ride. Other birds weren't so lucky. Suffocated from flying through the smoke, or simply exhausted, they fell from the sky and landed fluffed up on the road.

I would have liked to help them, and the other animals, too. There was room on Chainsaw for more passengers than just the honeyeater and me. But I was helpless to do anything. It was survival of the fittest, the fastest, the smartest. I hoped the slower creatures would find burrows to crawl into or streams to lie in. I hoped the fallen birds would get a second wind and take to the air again.

Most of all, I hoped that Chainsaw would keep going. Already he was huffing like a steam train.

For all his panting and blowing, I could still hear the roar of the fire. I could still feel its searing heat on the back of my neck. In the last few minutes, the hot, northerly wind seemed to have picked up, or perhaps it was the fire generating a wind of its own. Dust and smoke eddied around us. A sudden whirlwind nearly blew the honeyeater off Chainsaw's neck. For a moment the stricken bird hung upside down by one tiny twig-like foot, its eyes closed, its wings flapping feebly.

I grabbed the honeyeater and stuffed it gently into one of the badly shredded jacket pockets. There was nothing I could do for all the other animals and birds, but I could save this one. I *hoped* I could save it. Everything depended on Chainsaw.

Or did it? Over the roar of the flames, I became aware of another noise. It grew louder.

Thumpa thumpa thumpa thumpa!

A kangaroo? No, this was louder, more mechanical. It was a sound I'd heard on another occasion when my life hung in the balance.

I was saved!

⓳

FITTEST, FASTEST, SMARTEST

Chainsaw heard it too. His ears twitched. We both lifted our heads to the sky. *Thumpa thumpa thumpa.* The air seemed to quiver. I worked one hand free of the rope and raised it in the air, ready to wave when the helicopter came into view.

It didn't come into view. The sound passed right overhead. The helicopter couldn't have been more than fifty yards above the road, yet I saw nothing, not even a shadow. The smoke was too thick.

"Hey, I'm down here!" I yelled, waving my hand like an idiot. "I'm here! I'm here!"

I could have saved my breath. How was the pilot going to hear me over the noise the helicopter was making? The sound moved away.

Soon all I could hear was Chainsaw's huffing breath and the roar of flames. I tried to suppress my disappointment by telling myself that someone was looking for me. Nan and Pop must have reported me missing. It made me feel less alone to know a search was on. The helicopter would be back. It was only a matter of time before they found me.

We just had to keep ahead of the firestorm until that happened.

Chainsaw had slowed to a trot. His head was hanging, his breath came in great, wheezing gusts. Dust and soot clung to his sweaty coat. I leaned forward and patted his heaving ribcage. Poor old guy, he was just about done in. I wondered how much longer he could keep going. *It didn't matter,* I told myself. Soon the helicopter would find us.

Us? The helicopter wasn't looking for *us*, it was looking for *me*. Chainsaw would be left behind. It didn't seem right. The gutsy old bull had saved my life. But there was no way a helicopter could lift him out of the bushfire's path. It would take a special harness to do that. I would have to leave Chainsaw behind.

It wasn't fair.

Survival of the fittest, the fastest, the smartest. On that basis, Chainsaw had earned the right to live. He was fitter than me, and faster. Two out of three. As for intelligence, Chainsaw was smart enough to do what he'd been bred to do better than any other bull in the history of Australian rodeo – four hundred and twelve cowboys could attest to that. I'd only managed to ride him because he was blinded and confused by the smoke. And he was a hundred years old in bull years.

"I'll stick with you, old fella," I said.

But I was still listening for the helicopter as I spoke.

TWISTER

In the end, I didn't have to make a choice between staying with Chainsaw or being rescued. The helicopter pilot didn't find me. He wasn't even looking.

Ten minutes later the wind changed direction, and a gap opened in the smoke ahead. I saw a blue and white helicopter crossing the tea-colored sky with a large orange bucket dangling on cables beneath it. A faint haze of water trailed down from the bucket. The helicopter wasn't looking for me. It was conducting a water-bombing operation on the bushfire.

The opening in the smoke revealed something else as well. The ridges on either side of us – Copperhead Spur to our right, and the longer, lower ridge to our left – were both blazing from end to end.

I realized what had happened. Pushed along by the stronger winds up in the high country, the bushfire had raced ahead along both ridges, outflanking the valley we were following in a long, deadly pincer movement. Chainsaw and I were caught in the middle. But not trapped.

There was still a way out.

So far the fire hadn't moved down from the two ridges.

A narrow strip of unburned forest stretched ahead, all the way to the mouth of the valley. If we could get there before the flames moved down off the ridges, or the firestorm caught up with us from behind, we might still have a chance.

It seemed a very slim chance. Chainsaw had managed to put several hundred yards between us and the fire front, but the effort had taken a heavy toll. He was exhausted. His head hung, his breath whistled, and his hooves dragged. Still he trotted on.

Soot and embers fell around us like ugly black snow. We were the only ones on the road now. The other creatures had disappeared. Probably they were ahead. Or dead.

I found myself thinking about Susie, and wondering if she and the brumbies had made it to safety. But it was hard to keep my thoughts on anything other than the fire. I tried to shut out the crackle and roar of the approaching flames. They seemed to be gaining on us again. The wind on my back felt red hot. My eyes were running. My throat burned. I was dying of thirst and felt faint from heat and carbon monoxide poisoning. It must have been twice as bad for Chainsaw. I hoped he'd had a drink at the stream twenty minutes ago. The next twenty minutes, I sensed, would seal our fate one way or another.

There was a loud whoosh behind us. It was accompanied by a blast of heat that nearly blew me off Chainsaw's back. I turned and saw a terrifying sight. A tornado of twisting yellow flame raced towards us. It was as wide as the road and coiled several hundred yards into the sky, disappearing into the seething pall of ash and smoke.

Chainsaw must have seen the danger, too. He veered out of the twister's path and plunged into the forest beside the road. I had to duck to avoid low branches. The twister roared along the road behind us, showering us with a confetti of sparks and flaming debris.

I was clinging to Chainsaw's neck, much as I'd clung to Susie's earlier that day. Branches and vines and ferns swished past, tearing at my clothes, scratching my hands and feet and ankles. I couldn't sit up. I could do nothing to stop Chainsaw's panicked flight through the forest.

We seemed to be going downhill. The fiery twister was behind us somewhere. Now I could see a yellow wall of flame through the trees to my left. It was sweeping towards us on a half-mile-wide front. Since leaving the road, Chainsaw had taken a course running parallel to the firefront, rather than away from it. If he kept going in this direction, the bushfire would be on us within a minute. Perhaps less.

The silly old bull had totally lost it. He was going to kill us both!

21

OUT OF THE WOODS

It wasn't until I saw a shimmer of silver through the trees ahead that I realized I'd seriously misjudged Chainsaw. He knew exactly what he was doing. He wasn't killing us, he was saving our lives.

Nan and Pop had pointed out the turnoff to Platypus Dam a week earlier. Chainsaw hadn't waited to reach the turnoff. He'd smelled the water from Corcoran Road, and now he was making a beeline towards it. Nothing was going to stop him. Not even the fire.

It was very close now, only about forty or fifty yards to our left, and coming fast. The air was full of smoke and falling sparks. Already we had passed a number of small spot fires. Luckily, the forest was shielding us from the blast furnace heat of the main fire. Even so, it was incredibly hot. The air shimmered. The outlines of trees had become wobbly and blurred. I was gasping for breath. I felt nauseous from dehydration, dizzy from lack of oxygen.

Hugging Chainsaw's withers, I closed my eyes and hoped for the best. The big old bull huffed and puffed beneath me. He staggered, but recovered quickly and plowed on like a bulldozer towards the dam.

We made it. Thanks to Chainsaw, we beat the fire to the dam by about ten seconds. By the time the flames exploded through the trees along the bank, the bull and I were standing in the cool, oozy mud twenty yards from the shore. Only our eyes and noses were above the water.

It was muddy, but I didn't care. I drank and drank. A few yards away, Chainsaw was gulping like a sewer pump. It was a wonder the water level didn't drop!

After I'd taken the edge off my humungous thirst, I began to notice other eyes and noses around us. The dam was full of animals. There were kangaroos, wallabies, possums, wombats, goannas. Snakes!

One came wriggling through the water towards

me, probably looking for something to climb onto.
But I wasn't agreeable to that. I splashed water at it,
and it swam away.

I looked around for horses, but didn't see any.
The dam was quite large, and there was a lot smoke.
It was possible that Susie and the brumbies were at
the other end, where I couldn't see them. Birds had
gathered near the middle of the dam. There were
ducks, coots, grebes, swamp hens, a couple of herons
perched on a floating stick. I wondered what had
happened to the other birds, the ones that weren't
aquatic.

The honeyeaters!

In a panic, I ripped off the denim jacket and
opened the pocket in which I'd put the little green
and yellow honeyeater. It rolled out into my cupped
hand, a limp bundle of wet feathers. I'd forgotten
about it, and now it was dead. Poor little critter. It was
only a bird, but it would have been nice to have saved
it. Today wouldn't have been such a total disaster if I
had managed to do just one thing right. Instead, I'd
messed up just about everything.

A translucent eyelid slid open. A tiny claw came
slowly unclenched. The honeyeater sat up on my

hand and shook itself, settling its feathers into place. Then, in a flurry of damp wings, it darted low across the water and alighted on one of Chainsaw's horns. The bull flicked his ear. Otherwise he seemed unconcerned.

I looked at the pair of them, the bull and the honeyeater, and smiled. It felt like the first time I'd smiled in about a century. The last few hours had *seemed* like a century. But they were over now. As the saying goes, I was out of the woods.

ⓩ

... AND INTO THE FIRE

I heard the helicopter again.

As the sound grew steadily louder, my heart began pumping. It was coming to Platypus Dam! The pilot needed more water to fight the fire, and he was going to refill his bucket from the very dam where I had taken refuge. I was saved!

I couldn't see the helicopter because there was too much smoke. The bushfire completely encircled the dam. Whichever way I looked, towering yellow flames leapt into the sky. Banks of choking brown smoke rolled out across the water. I hoped the pilot could find his way through. He wouldn't bring his machine down if he couldn't see the dam – that would be too dangerous.

Thumpa thumpa thumpa thumpa!

The helicopter drew closer. It thundered out over the lake and passed directly overhead. I strained my eyes, but all I could see was smoke. The sound moved away to my left, then I heard the rotor beat quicken as the helicopter climbed.

"Come back! It's down here! The dam's right here!" I screamed, waving Adam's jacket above my head, aware that I was wasting my energy.

I was desperate. If the helicopter went away, I would be trapped in the dam until the fire burned out. And then I would have to rely on Chainsaw to carry me to safety. I groaned at the thought of having to ride him again.

Thumpa thumpa thumpa thumpa!

The helicopter was coming back. It had flown in a circle and returned to the dam. A large shadow loomed overhead. I felt a powerful, downward draft on my wet hair and face. A hole appeared in the smoke, blown open by the helicopter's rotor, and the big orange bucket came swinging down. It flopped into the water halfway between me and the middle of the dam. Ducks and water birds scattered in all directions.

The helicopter came into view. It was hovering about thirty yards above the mostly submerged bucket. It was a blue and white Bell Jet Ranger – the same model that had rescued me and my cousin from a crocodile-infested river in the Northern Territory. Luckily there were no crocodiles here. There were snakes, though. And a bushfire. And a tired old bull who looked like he could quite happily spend the rest of his life in the dam.

I waved Adam's jacket, I yelled my lungs out. But the Jet Ranger was facing the wrong direction. The pilot couldn't see me.

Tossing the jacket aside, I began swimming out towards the helicopter. I was frantic. It was unthinkable that it would leave without me. I had been through too much to be abandoned now.

I reached the bucket and grabbed hold of the wobbly rim with one hand. I waved my free hand desperately at the Jet Ranger. It was right above me.

I was moments too late. There was a small window in the floor of the helicopter which allowed the pilot to look through when he was filling the bucket. But the bucket was full, and he had just turned his attention back to the controls. He tipped the nose forward and put the Jet Ranger into a steep climb.

I should have let go. But, by the time I realized what was happening, I was already sixty feet above the water, dangling one-handed from the bucket's rim. It was too far to drop. Straining against the multiplied G-forces of the helicopter's climb, I clawed my other hand up over the side of the bucket for a more secure hold. It was lucky that I did, because as soon as we were higher than the flaming treetops, the pilot executed a ninety degree pedal turn, swinging the bucket in a wide, gut-churning arc that nearly flung me into the firestorm. Somehow I held on. Just. The bucket was made of heavy nylon. Its narrow rim sagged down where I gripped it, causing a steady stream of water to spill onto my face. Dangling by my fingertips five or six hundred feet over the raging bushfire, I was slowly drowning!

The bucket resembled an upside-down tepee, held open at the top by a circular metal frame. Four steel cables were attached to the frame, connecting it to the helicopter.

I grabbed one of the cables and hooked one leg over the lip of the bucket. Trembling with effort, I hauled myself up. At the point of balance, my knee slipped, and I went headfirst into the water. I came up spitting and spluttering, gripped the edge and collapsed breathless against the side.

I'd made it! I was safe. Bubbles rose all around me. Air was leaking in somewhere down near my feet. It was like being in a flying spa.

I thrust my chin over the side and blinked the water from my eyes. We were clear of the smoke cloud, flying along the side of a burning ridge. As I took in the view, the truth hit me like a hammer blow. I *wasn't* safe. Pretty soon the pilot was going to dump the water onto that fire. And I would go with it!

I had to attract his attention. But how? The Jet Ranger was traveling fast, trailing the bucket behind it. Even if the pilot looked down, he wouldn't see me.

I would have to climb the cables. Was it possible? Would I be able to climb the cables using just my hands and my unbroken, though badly gashed, right foot? I had to. My life depended on it.

Careful not to look down, I gripped two of the thin steel cables, placed the toes of my right foot on the bucket's narrow rim and hauled myself out of the water.

Fear of heights isn't something you can control. You can be the bravest person in the world when it comes to other things – riding bulls, for example, or staring down humungous spiders – and then freak out at the view from the top of a stepladder. I'm actually pretty good at stepladders now, but fire buckets dangling from helicopters? No way. Here I was balanced on the edge on the toes of one foot. My hands were clamped around the two skinny steel cables. I was holding on so tight my knuckles were white. The wind was whistling in my ears and tearing at my dripping wet clothes. And I couldn't move. I couldn't climb the cables, and I couldn't climb back down. I was frozen.

My timing was bad. I was standing on the edge of the bucket when the pilot put the helicopter into a long, steep dive. My stomach climbed into my rib cage.

I knew it was a bad idea but I couldn't stop myself. I looked down.

Oh!

We were dropping into the mouth of a volcano!

Only it wasn't a volcano. It was a dead-end gully totally surrounded by fire. From my perspective it looked like a scene from the end of the world. And it was the end. For me. I think my eyelids were the only part of my body that I could still control. I snapped them closed. It was better not to look.

Heat. I began to feel warm. Then hot. The air was on fire. Smoke burned in my nostrils. I stopped breathing. My whole system closed down, except for the little voice in my brain.

I don't want to die! it shrieked.

Suddenly, my stomach slumped back down to where it was supposed to be. We had stopped descending. But my troubles were far from over. I was no longer going down, I was going forward. Straight towards the source of the unbelievable heat. Orange glowed through my eyelids.

This is it, I thought.

Above me, there was a sudden change in the engine note as the helicopter went into a climb. Its rotor clawed at the air with a deafening *thwap thwap thwap thwap*.

The world tipped and began to swing like a giant pendulum.

Enormous G-forces gripped me. I felt my toes slip off the bucket's rim, the cables sliding through my hands. I felt myself falling …

My eyes snapped open.

I was *inside* the fire!

Burning trees whirled around me. I was surrounded by gusts of yellow flame, explosions of sparks, whipping, red-hot branches. Yet none of it touched me. I felt peaceful and oddly cool. I was looking at the fire from another dimension – from a dream, perhaps. I seemed to be underwater, inside a giant bubble looking out at the flaming inferno, completely engulfed by fire, yet not burning.

Twang!

I was dropping. My stomach flew all the way up into my ribcage again. Down, down, down I went, helpless in my plummeting bubble, smashing through the trees in a whirl of flames and sparks.

Then, with an impact that seemed to stop the whole universe, I hit the ground.

REUNION

I found out later what had happened.

The helicopter pilot's name was Vin Alison. He had flown down into the burning gully to bomb it with water. When he looked through the porthole in the Jet Ranger's floor to line up his drop, he saw me standing on the edge of the bucket. The sight was so unexpected, so weird, that it took him a few moments to grasp what he was seeing. In those few moments, things went horribly wrong.

The helicopter was swooping into the burning gully at roughly fifty knots, which is fifty-five miles per hour if you're in a car. Vin had been about to level out and begin his water drop when he saw me.

By the time he gathered his wits, the Jet Ranger was much lower than it should have been and heading straight for the wall of flame. Vin put it into a power climb, but he was too late. The helicopter was carrying a thousand-pound payload of water, not to mention one hundred thirty pounds of stowaway, and it didn't rise fast enough. The bucket smashed into the burning treetops and became entangled in the branches. When Vin tried to free it, the cables snagged on one of the Jet Ranger's landing skids, and the helicopter went into a partial rollover. By this stage, Vin thought I was dead. He didn't realize I had fallen *into* the bucket and not off it, so he hit the emergency cable-release in a last-ditch effort to save himself and the Jet Ranger.

I heard it flying away. I wasn't sure what had happened. It was only later that I would work it out. The water in the bucket cushioned my fall. Now I found myself sitting in a tangle of cables and wet orange nylon, with solid ground beneath me. I was unhurt, apart from my throbbing right foot, which had lost its makeshift bandage some time in the last half hour. At least the bleeding had stopped. My broken foot was completely numb.

A flaming branch landed on the wet ground beside me, sending up a hiss of steam. It woke me up to the grim truth of my situation. I had survived the fall from the helicopter, only to end up back in the bushfire. Above and behind me, the whole sky seemed to be on fire, yet the ground all around me was damp and steaming. I saw an opening in the flames ahead. On hands and knees, I crawled between the black steaming tree trunks and out into the open.

I was in a narrow gully. Bushes and small trees smoldered here and there along the steep, rocky sides. Higher up, fire ringed the sky. Ash and sparks rained down. So far, the gully floor seemed to have escaped the flames. Using a stick as a crutch, I hobbled slowly into the gully through the waist-high ferns and bracken. The foliage felt damp. *Why was it damp?* I wondered. The bucket was at least forty yards away – no way could its contents have splashed this far.

I stopped in my tracks. Stones crunched. A stick snapped. There was something in the gully ahead of me.

"Hello? Is anyone there?" I called. As if it would be human.

I heard a thump, followed by a low coughing

sound. Whatever it was, it sounded big. I looked nervously behind me at the burning trees. Some of the ferns at the side of the gully were smoking. I had to go forward.

In my brief glimpse of it from the air, I had seen that the gully had a dead-end. Whatever was ahead of me would be trapped. I knew that some animals could become quite dangerous if cornered. I'd heard stories of kangaroos attacking people and inflicting serious injuries. But I couldn't go back. The fire was behind me. I pushed aside my fears and hobbled nervously forward.

More noises. The shuffle of feet.

Sweating now, I eased a fern frond to one side. No more than five yards away, a shaggy gray horse raised its head and snorted. It cantered up the gully and joined a mob of ten or eleven other horses gathered near the vertical rock wall at the end. Brumbies. Twelve of them. They stood watching me, their eyes wide with alarm.

I was only interested in one of them – a small palomino mare that was standing slightly apart from the others.

"Susie!" I called.

24

THROUGH THE FIRE

Here's something else I found out later.

Vin Alison, the helicopter pilot, had been trying to save Susie and the brumbies. He had spotted them trapped in the gully on one of his earlier fire-bombing runs. Vin's an animal lover. Instead of continuing on to the top of Copperhead Spur, where he was supposed to be fighting the bushfire, he dropped his load of water on the burning trees hemming in the horses. He came back twice more to douse the fire-encircled gully. On his fourth trip, he brought me along.

There was a small spring at the head of the gully. It had nearly dried up over the long, hot summer, but there was still a tiny pool, less than three feet across, where the water trickled down the rocky wall and collected at the bottom. The smell of water must have attracted the brumbies and Susie as they fled from the bushfire. They had filed up into the gully and become trapped.

In total, Vin and his helicopter had dropped five hundred gallons of water on the trees and bracken at the gully entrance. He had slowed the fire down, but he hadn't stopped it altogether. It was moving up the gully floor as the bracken ahead dried, advancing towards us in a wide yellow wave. Soon it would reach the bracken that hadn't been touched by Vin's bombing runs. It was brown and tinder-dry, and it came up to the top of the gully. The horses and I would be caught in a firestorm. Our only hope was to get out of the gully before the flames reached the dry bracken. And there was only one way out – through the fire.

My broken foot was too sore to put in the stirrup, but that was hardly a handicap to someone who had ridden bareback on a bull. I wheeled Susie around behind the brumbies and tried to push them down the gully. They didn't want to go. After only a few yards, they broke ranks and rushed back past us on both sides. I didn't blame them. Between us and the gully entrance was a sea of flames. Soon that sea would become a tsunami, and then there would be no escape.

I tried again. I shouted and waved and wheeled Susie back and forth behind the nervous, flighty brumbies. Slowly, they began to edge towards the fire. I was just beginning to think we were getting somewhere when the first of the dry bracken fronds near the gully wall suddenly flared up, sending a tower of crackling flame ten feet into the air. One or two of the brumbies whinnied, then the whole herd turned and galloped past Susie deeper into the gully. There was nothing we could do to stop them.

I glanced anxiously at the fire. A second flare-up had occurred in the dry bracken on the other side of the gully. The flames jumped and crackled as the two arms of the fire moved towards each other. We had about a minute, I estimated, before they joined and became an impenetrable conflagration.

One more try, I thought, riding back towards the brumbies. If they broke away again, Susie and I would have to leave them to their fiery fate and save ourselves.

Make your surroundings work for you, I remembered.

Trailing down over the rocks at the head of the gully were several long tendrils of vine. I leaned out of the saddle and yanked one free. Using my teeth, I stripped off the leaves. Twirling the twelve-foot vine over my head, then swinging it in a wide loop, I flicked it with my forearm and wrist. *Crack!* As loud as a gunshot. I tried it again, this time aiming the makeshift whip above the head of the nearest wild horse. *Crack!*

The terrified brumbies bunched close together and looked at me with nervous eyes. I whooped loudly, cracked the vine again, and they were off.

Thirteen horses running full tilt, we charged through the burning bracken like a single, many-hoofed animal. The flames seemed to part ahead of the great galloping beast, the air filled with spinning sparks and clods of flying earth. I cracked my whip again as we burst out the other side. We flew between the steaming trunks of two trees Vin Alison had doused, swooped through a tunnel of black eucalyptus whose crowns still flared and smoldered, then shot out into the smoky, burned-out landscape beyond.

We had made it!

THE BOY FROM SNOWY RIVER

Before too long, we came to a road, and the tired brumbies stopped galloping. I kept them bunched together. The wild horses were black with soot, but none seemed burned or injured. One or two of them looked at me sitting on Susie's back. They seemed lost and uncertain in this strange, blackened countryside that before the fire had been their home range. Now not a speck of green showed anywhere. There was nothing for them to eat, nowhere for them to hide.

I cracked the whip and moved the herd steadily along the road between the smoking trees. I was taking them somewhere green.

The wind had changed from a northerly to an easterly in the last hour. No smoke was blowing over from the far side of Copperhead Spur. I reckoned Nan and Pop's farm had escaped the fire.

We passed a turnoff and a badly burnt sign. All I could read was *PLATYP*. It was enough to tell me where we were. Through the skeletal forest on my left, I glimpsed the distant shine of water. Chainsaw would be safe until Pop came to collect him in the truck. The other truck, the one Adam and Pig-eyes had used, would be destroyed by now. As would Adam's cell phone.

I still remembered Mr. Cameron's number and the name of his farm. The Jindabyne Rustlers would soon be getting a visit from the police.

I had been right about the fire. The wind change had pushed it down off Copperhead Spur. It had burned across the path of the main fire front, creating a natural firebreak.

In the late afternoon, I herded the brumbies around the foot of the spur and into green farmland.

Far ahead, I saw a familiar four-wheel drive approaching along the dusty road. I stood high on one stirrup and waved it back. Nan, who was driving, got the idea. She did a U-turn and stayed a couple of hundred yards ahead of the brumbies all the way back to the farm. I slowed the herd down while Pop opened the gate. He climbed back in, and Nan drove around behind the cattle yards where the vehicle wouldn't spook the brumbies.

I knew they had a hundred questions to ask me – and I had a *thousand* things to tell them – but the talking could wait.

Susie and I had a job to finish.

Nan and Pop stood behind the rails and watched. I must have looked a sight in my burned and tattered clothes, with my bare, black-and-blue feet and my frizzy, scorched hair. I was bone-tired, every part of me felt scraped or battered or burned or bruised, but I sat tall in the saddle on Susie's back. Swinging the whip in a high, wide arc, I cracked it loudly and sent the twelve wild horses trotting ahead of us into the bull paddock.

I felt like the man from Snowy River.

About the author

Born in New Zealand, Justin D'Ath is one of twelve children. He came to Australia in 1971 to study for missionary priesthood. After three years, he left the seminary in the dead of night and spent two years roaming Australia on a motorcycle. While doing that he began writing for motorcycle magazines. He published his first novel for adults in 1989. This was followed by numerous award-winning short stories, also for adults. Justin has worked in a sugar mill, on a cattle station, in a mine, on an island, in a laboratory, built cars, picked fruit, driven forklifts and taught writing for twelve years. He wrote his first children's book in 1996. To date he has published twenty-three books. He has two children, two grandchildren, and one dog.

www.justindath.com

3/2011